Bad Boy, Billy!

Gerald Rose

CAMBRIDGE
UNIVERSITY PRESS

One day, I went into the field to pick some apples.
I forgot to shut the gate.

Billy ran out through the gate and into our garden.

"Come back, Billy!" I shouted.

"Don't eat the washing!" I shouted,

but Billy liked socks.

"Bad boy, Billy!" I said.

"Shoo! Get out of the garden!" I shouted,

but Billy liked carrots.

"Bad boy, Billy!" I said.

Billy ran out into the road.

"Don't eat the letters!" shouted the postman,

but Billy liked letters.
"Bad boy, Billy!" I said.

9

Nobody could catch Billy.

I ran back to the field to get the apples.

I gave one to Billy.

"Come on, Billy," I said.

Billy followed me all the way back to the field.

This time I shut the gate.

"Good boy, Billy!"